Capybara Learning to Swi

Max Marshall

Capybara Learning to Swim

First edition. June 27, 2024.

This book was written partially using AI content in the text and illustrations.

CAPYBARA
LEARNING
TO SWIM
Max Marshall

Table of Contents

Description

Initially in a lush rainforest, there lived a curious and kind-hearted capybara named Leonardo. All the animals admired him for his soft fur and gentle nature. But there was one thing that made Leonardo feel different from his friends—he was afraid of water! Determined to conquer his fears, Leonardo embarked on an exciting adventure with his trusty squirrel friend, Sammy. Together, they sought the guidance of wise old turtles and mischievous otters who taught them the secrets of swimming. With each lesson, Leonardo's confidence grew, and he discovered that beneath the surface, a whole new world awaited him. Through bravery, perseverance, and the power of friendship, Leonardo transformed from a timid capybara into a fearless swimmer, inspiring others to embrace their own fears and dive into new experiences. This delightful fairy tale celebrates the magic of overcoming obstacles and finding strength within oneself, reminding young readers that even the smallest creatures can achieve great things.

About the Author

Max Marshall creates stories that transport readers to far-off lands, immersing them in rich cultures and inviting them to experience the full spectrum of human emotion.

Nestled within the pages of countless masterpieces lies a writer whose name evokes thoughts of passion, creativity, and boundless imagination.

With an elegant command of language and a deep understanding of the human soul, this writer creates characters whose triumphs and struggles resonate deeply with readers of all ages. Whether exploring the complexities of love and loss or delving into the depths of the human psyche, this writer's prose is as beautiful as it is insightful, revealing truths that stir the heart and inspire the soul.

Chapter 1: A Capybara afraid of Water

Lyona, the capybara, had a secret. A big, squishy, terrifying secret. Lyona was afraid of water. Not just a little bit afraid, but so afraid that her heart would pound like a drum and her fur would prickle like a porcupine's quills at the mere sight of a puddle.

Now, being a capybara, this was a problem. Capybaras, after all, are known for their love of water. They are excellent swimmers, often found splashing about in rivers, lakes, and even enjoying a good soak in the sunshine. But Lyona, well, she just preferred lounging in the sun on the dry, sandy bank.

One warm, sunny morning, a group of playful otters, led by the mischievous Chuck, were frolicking in a small, clear puddle. They were diving and swirling, their sleek bodies like silver streaks in the water. Lyona watched them with a mixture of envy and dread. Oh, how she wanted to join in the fun! But just the thought of dipping even a single toe sent chills down her spine.

-Come on, Lyona!

- Chuck hollered, his voice as bubbly as the water he was splashing in.

-Don't be a scaredy-cat! Swimming is fun!

-Lyona tried to muster her courage. She carefully dipped one of her large, webbed feet into the puddle, testing the water. A shiver ran through her. The water was so cold!

-It's not so bad, is it?

- Chuck called out, trying to coax her closer. He moved his tiny paws with exaggerated motions, pretending to row a boat. Lyona couldn't help but giggle. Chuck's funny little dance made the fear in her heart feel a bit less prickly.

Lyona knew she needed to learn how to swim, but she also knew she needed to do it at her own pace. Maybe she could just start by putting both of her front paws in the water... then maybe a back paw... With Chuck's encouragement and a few playful giggles, Lyona began her journey to conquer her fear, one tiny step – or paw - at a time.

Chapter 2: Panic and Playfulness of Otters

Lyona, emboldened by the laughter and Chuck's encouragement, decided to take a leap. A literal leap! She took a deep breath and with a nervous giggle, plunged both her front paws into the cool water of the puddle.

-See! It's not so bad, is it? - Chuck chuckled, bobbing beside her.

-Just relax and let the water support you.

Feeling brave, Lyona tried a new technique. She remembered the graceful swan, always gliding effortlessly across the lake, and attempted to imitate it by flipping onto her back. The sun felt warm on her fur as she drifted, and for a moment, everything was good. But then, she forgot the advice Chuck had given her, and fear began to gnaw at her.

-Oh, no,

- Lyona panicked,

-I'm stuck! I can't get back up!

-

Panic filled her little heart, causing her to flail wildly with her paws, only pushing her deeper into the water. Water rushed into her nostrils, and she struggled to keep her head above the surface.

-Help! Help! - Lyona choked out, her voice filled with terror.

Just then, a boisterous troupe of playful otters, seemingly out of nowhere, dashed past Lyona. They zoomed through the puddle like a streak of shimmering, wet fur. They bumped into each other, rolled and splashed, showering Lyona with icy spray. The sudden, chaotic movement completely disoriented Lyona, amplifying her fear.

With a frantic lunge, Lyona propelled herself out of the water, landing with a loud

-sploosh - back onto the sandy bank. She sputtered and coughed, trembling with relief and exhaustion.

Her adventure into the world of swimming was a near-disaster. The water had turned into a giant, watery monster, ready to devour her. Chuck, seeing her distress, swam back and cautiously circled around her. He gently nudged her with his nose.

-Are you alright? - he asked, his voice tinged with concern.

-It's just a puddle! Come on, let's try again. You can do it!

-Lyona, drenched and breathless, took another look at the playful otters still splashing in the puddle. They looked so happy, so confident, so free! Perhaps, one day, she too could be like them. But for now, her heart needed a moment to recover from the fear.

Chapter 3: The Grace of the Swan

Lyona sat huddled on the warm bank, her heart still thumping like a drum. The playful otters had disappeared into the woods, leaving her alone with her fear. But Lyona was not alone. Across the lake, perched gracefully on the surface, was a beautiful white swan with feathers as white as freshly fallen snow. The swan, known throughout the forest as Serena, seemed to move without effort, gliding across the water with such poise and confidence that Lyona couldn't help but be mesmerized.

Lyona had never felt comfortable around Serena, as the swan had a certain elegance that made Lyona feel self-conscious about her clumsy waddle. Yet, today, as Serena swam effortlessly through the water, she became an unexpected source of inspiration for Lyona.

-Isn't she beautiful? - Chuck chirped, joining Lyona on the bank.

Lyona nodded, mesmerized.

-It looks so easy, doesn't it?

Chuck sighed and scratched his head with his little paw.

-I'm not sure what Serena's secret is. I've never seen anything like it.

-She's so light! - Lyona exclaimed,

-like she's barely touching the water.

Chuck glanced at her with a curious smile.

-Come, let's try a little experiment.

- He waddled over to a large sheet that had been used to cover the picnic basket earlier that morning. With his little paw, he pulled a corner of the sheet into the puddle.

-Imagine this sheet is a giant, flat bird, like Serena,

- he said, pressing down on the sheet with his tiny paw.

-The water is holding it up. That's because water can push back. That's what makes it feel like we're floating!

-Lyona, curious, hopped closer.

-Float? Like, a feather floating on air? - she asked, feeling a spark of hope inside her.

-Exactly! - Chuck grinned,

-Our bodies can float on the water. That's why you almost didn't drown, Lyona! -

-Oh.

- Lyona pondered this new information.

-It was my panicking that made me sink? - she asked.

-Exactly!

- Chuck confirmed.

-Relaxation is key. We can learn from Serena how to use buoyancy, how to use the water to help us.

As they watched Serena glide effortlessly, a flicker of courage began to rise within Lyona. Maybe with a little practice, maybe by trusting the water, she too could learn to float like the graceful swan.

The journey would not be easy, and Lyona's fear was still there. But with Chuck's kindness and Serena's inspiring grace, she was ready to take another leap – a cautious, tentative leap towards conquering the fear that held her back.

Chapter 4: Warning

The next day, Lyona found herself at the edge of a flowing river, a little nervous but determined. With Chuck at her side, she tried to follow Serena's example, attempting to float on her back like the swan. She carefully slid into the water, keeping her paws close to her sides. This time, the water seemed less frightening. It felt cool and buoyant.

-You're doing great, Lyona! - Chuck called from the shore, watching with a reassuring smile.

Lyona, with a cautious glance toward the other side of the river, decided she was feeling brave enough to take a step closer.

-Watch me!

- she proudly announced. With a determined heave, she kicked off the bank with her powerful back legs, sending a spray of water cascading onto Chuck. Lyona paddled slowly towards the middle of the river.

The current wasn't strong enough to sweep her away.

-See, Chuck, I'm not that bad!

- Lyona declared, a bit too proudly for her liking. She was pleased to see Chuck watching with approval. Lyona, enjoying this newfound confidence, decided to push herself a little further.

-Hold on, Lyona,

- she whispered, almost to herself.

-Think about Serena!

- With a big, excited lunge, she kicked hard off the bank.

But she didn't manage to stay afloat like the elegant swan.

Her efforts, instead of a smooth gliding motion, were a mix of clumsy kicks and flailing arms. It made her look more like a wobbly duck, waddling rather than gliding.

-Lyona! - Chuck shrieked.

-Be careful! This part of the river is a bit trickier.

He swiveled his little head around and looked at Lyona with concerned eyes.

-You need to be extra cautious with the current here.

-Before Lyona could react, a grumpy voice rumbled from the bank. It was the Old River Turtle, an elder of the river, with a moss-covered shell as wide as Lyona's back. He stared down at Lyona with disapproving, yellow eyes.

-Young Capybara,

- he rumbled, his voice as deep as a storm cloud.

-Don't be so reckless. This current is no joke. It will carry you far away if you aren't careful.

-The Old River Turtle's warning, spoken with such severity, brought Lyona's wild swimming to a halt. She sank her hooves into the sandy bank, letting the current sweep her backward towards the shore. Lyona was relieved. The Old River Turtle, though grumpy, was wise. His words reminded her that she needed to approach this journey to becoming a swimmer with more caution, more respect for the river, and with more patience.

Chapter 5: Holding Your Breath and Sinking Pebbles

Lyona sat on the bank of the river, watching the current ripple by with a mix of curiosity and caution. The Old River Turtle's warning was still fresh in her mind, a reminder that this powerful river was not something to be taken lightly. But the memory of Serena gliding effortlessly across the lake, of Chuck's encouragement, and the excitement of feeling the water beneath her had not completely disappeared.

Lyona wanted to learn to swim, but the fear was still there, holding her back. To face her fear, she needed a plan.

-Chuck, - Lyona said, her voice low,

-what if I tried holding my breath underwater?

Chuck looked up from the smooth stones he was arranging on a flat piece of driftwood.

-Why would you do that? - he asked, tilting his head in confusion.

-Well, Serena dives deep down to find reeds, - Lyona explained,

-If I want to learn to swim, I should probably practice holding my breath underwater, right?

-Chuck chuckled, a bit amused by her reasoning.

-Serena's different. She can hold her breath for much longer than any of us! - He said.

-Maybe we should start by trying to dive for some of these pebbles! -

With his tiny paw, Chuck gently pushed a smooth, river-worn stone toward the edge of the bank. Lyona's curiosity piqued.

-Dive?

- she questioned, surprised by this suggestion.

-How would we do that?

-Watch!

- Chuck shouted, plunging head first into the water. Lyona gasped. Chuck seemed to have disappeared! A moment later, he popped his head up from the surface.

-Well, dive!

- Chuck encouraged, a little excitedly.

-Don't forget what we practiced last time. Trust the water!

Hesitantly, Lyona took a deep breath. She visualized Serena gracefully diving to the bottom of the river. Then, with a push of her strong back legs, she plunged into the water, holding her breath as she went down.

For a brief moment, it was magical. She was like a fish in water. Then she started to panic, feeling her breath escape. Lyona popped her head back up.

-Oops, just a second, - she laughed nervously.

-You did good! It's more than a second! - Chuck reassured, placing a soft paw on Lyona's shoulder.

-Let's try another pebble. See how many seconds you can manage! Maybe we can even work our way up to a minute!

-

And so, with Chuck collecting more and more pebbles, Lyona spent the afternoon learning how to hold her breath and feeling her fear diminish as she slowly increased the amount of time she spent underwater. Her confidence started to grow, and with each new pebble, she realized that mastering swimming might be more achievable than she first thought.

Chapter 6: Dreams of Salvation and Inspiring Stories

The day after Lyona's dive training, a restless night awaited her. She tossed and turned in her bed of soft grass, plagued by a terrifying dream.

In the dream, the water, instead of feeling cool and buoyant, was a cold, unforgiving darkness. She felt herself pulled under, her paws struggling to find the surface, the water in her lungs like heavy stones, threatening to drown her.

Lyona woke with a gasp, drenched in a cold sweat, her heart pounding in her chest. She could still feel the weight of the water on her, the fear so real it felt like a bad taste on her tongue. She wished for sunlight, for the warmth of the sun on her fur, for the reassuring presence of her friend.

A gentle tap on her shoulder brought Lyona out of her nightmarish haze. Chuck stood beside her, concern in his big, black eyes.

-Are you alright, Lyona?

- Chuck asked, his voice soft as the early morning breeze.

Lyona sniffled, wiping away the sweat from her forehead.

-Just a bad dream, - she confessed.

-Oh, you must have had a terrible dream, - Chuck said, sympathizing.

Chuck settled himself next to Lyona, comforting her as she continued to tremble, her fear a cold hand clutching her heart.

-I know it's scary, - Chuck said.

-But even though I am an otter, I once had a friend who was scared of the water. He was just like you! And he learned how to swim. -

Lyona looked at Chuck, intrigued.

-It was an amazing story! - Chuck announced excitedly.

-He was called Pedro, the famous capybara swimmer, and he was the fastest capybara in all of the wetlands! No one had ever swum the wide River Canyon, but one day, Pedro decided to do it!

Chuck's story filled Lyona with awe. She sat mesmerized, picturing a small capybara like herself but with an unyielding spirit, tackling an incredibly challenging feat.

-He jumped into the water, with a powerful stroke!

- Chuck narrated, with wide eyes.

-He braved the strongest current, all the while feeling terrified. He had to face every fear to conquer that mighty River Canyon! -

-And he did it?, - Lyona asked, still awed by the story.

Chuck nodded.

-Yes! His victory was incredible! And remember, he used to be terrified! If he can do it, you can do it too.

-Just like you, Lyona, - Chuck added, reassuringly,

-You are not alone.

Lyona realized that the water didn't have to be a source of terror, that even with the deepest fear, the possibility of reaching incredible heights existed. The tale of Pedro, the famous capybara swimmer, was proof that anything was possible. If he could brave a raging current and reach victory, Lyona could also find courage in her journey.

Lyona took a deep breath. As the first rays of the sun crept over the forest, she took a comforting, comforting sigh, realizing that even a small, fearful capybara, with a friend like Chuck and a spirit like Pedro, could be a fearless swimmer one day.

Chapter 7: Mud Practice and Happy Splashes

Armed with newfound courage, Lyona was ready for a new challenge. With Pedro, the famous capybara swimmer, as her inspiration, she resolved to face her fears head-on. She would start with a less frightening training ground.

After all, Lyona reasoned, water wasn't the only thing that offered resistance, and that's what she was struggling to adapt to. Her big webbed feet were perfect for moving through water, but the challenge came when she tried to keep her head above it. Perhaps practice was needed before she ventured back to the river.

That day, Lyona chose to train in the muddy bank of the river, a place with soft, wet soil perfect for imitating water. Chuck was busy teaching a younger otter how to fish, so Lyona decided to practice on her own.

She took a deep breath and imagined she was submerged in water, feeling its resistance pushing against her fur. Then, she took a leap and imagined a powerful stroke, just like Pedro. She moved her big, webbed feet, trying to imitate the kick. The mud clung to her fur and her paws sank into the soil, but Lyona continued, pretending the mud was water.

For a long while, she moved through the mud with determined concentration. Lyona focused on her form, kicking with her back legs and reaching out with her front paws, striving to move with as much grace as Serena.

It was surprisingly effective. After a few minutes of clumsy movements, her clumsy kicks evolved into rhythmic movements that gave her the illusion of swimming. The thick mud created a resistance, but also allowed for a safer learning experience. Lyona even found that her feet weren't as awkward in the mud as she had initially imagined, giving her a little confidence boost.

Suddenly, a happy commotion echoed across the bank. Lyona looked up to see a group of little capybara children giggling and splashing in a small, shallow section of the river. She watched them with a curious heart, amazed at how carefree and unworried they were about the water. They looked happy and comfortable as they dipped, splashed, and kicked. They were even jumping and diving!

-Water isn't so terrible! - Lyona thought, watching the playful group.

The sight of the young capybaras reminded Lyona that, just like them, she, too, could learn to love water. Seeing them in their joyful splashes, Lyona realised that the water was not a monstrous beast that threatened to devour her, but rather, a playful companion. And maybe, just maybe, it was time to re-enter the river.

With a new wave of courage surging through her, Lyona felt ready for her next adventure. This time, with a smile on her face, she headed for the river, determined to learn how to be a brave and fearless swimmer like Pedro, the capybara, and those playful young capybaras.

Chapter 8: Rainbow Shell and Shallow Riverbed

The sun was setting, painting the sky with warm hues of orange and pink as Lyona made her way to a little pond tucked away in a secluded part of the forest. This wasn't a big river like the one she'd tried to swim in before. It was small, quiet, and incredibly clear, with the bottom clearly visible. The pond was shallow and seemed almost inviting, with sunlight shimmering on the water's surface. It looked like a miniature mirror, reflecting the colorful world above.

-Do you think I could swim here, Chuck?

- Lyona asked cautiously, dipping one paw into the cool, still water. The fear, while still present, felt a bit less menacing.

Chuck, sitting beside her, was carefully placing his paw onto a smooth, black rock in the pond.

-It looks safe enough, - Chuck responded.

-The water here isn't as strong as the river. You could easily touch the bottom!

-Lyona's eyes widened.

-Touch the bottom? Really?

-Of course, it's quite shallow! - Chuck confirmed. He reached out and carefully dipped his nose into the pond, showing Lyona that the water wasn't deeper than the length of his snout.

-Come on, Lyona. You could even try diving down to find something cool. -

Emboldened by Chuck's reassurance and excited by the prospect of touching the pond's bottom, Lyona carefully dipped her toes into the crystal clear water, slowly but steadily, advancing her feet closer to the shore. She held her breath and cautiously pushed off the sandy edge with a little kick, testing the water's resistance.

-It's not so scary after all!

- she laughed to herself. She started to float gently, allowing her webbed feet to glide through the water.

-See! I'm doing it!

- she called out to Chuck.

With a splash and a little smile, Lyona started to look around at the different plants and stones underneath the pond. They were clearly visible due to the clarity of the water. She noticed beautiful river pebbles in a rainbow of colors, gleaming at her from the pond floor. There were so many colours!

-There's something really pretty! - Lyona gasped as she spotted a magnificent shell with hues of blue, pink, and gold swirling like a miniature rainbow. Lyona wanted to get closer to see the shell, but she realized she wasn't sure how to dive down without disturbing the tranquility of the water.

-Let me help! - Chuck chirped. He had been carefully observing her, watching as Lyona's initial apprehension transformed into playful discovery. He offered to assist.

Lyona felt so comfortable now that the water didn't feel like a daunting monster anymore. Instead, it was a mysterious, wondrous world. With a gentle splash and a bit of encouragement from Chuck, Lyona began her underwater exploration.

As Lyona's nose reached the bottom of the pond, she squeezed the shell softly, feeling the coolness of its surface. She turned it over in her small paw, admiring the magnificent rainbow of colors and the delicate details of the smooth shell. She had discovered a little treasure!

-It's beautiful,

- she whispered in awe, her voice bubbling with excitement, as she held it close. This experience opened Lyona's eyes to a whole new world.

As the sun dipped further below the horizon, bathing the pond in golden hues, Lyona swam with increasing confidence. The shallow riverbed became a playground of discoveries, the water no longer a source of fear, but a new exciting and mesmerizing world of wonder and possibility.

Chapter 9: Small Steps and Songs of Bravery

The following days were filled with a newfound purpose. Lyona was determined to turn her fear of water into a love for it. Chuck was an amazing teacher, always encouraging and patient.

Every day, Lyona and Chuck visited the shallow part of the river.

-Let's take just one small step every day, Lyona, - Chuck advised, always reminding her about her courage. He would wait at the bank, smiling and cheering, his voice as bubbly as the water, while she took one step, two steps, three steps, slowly making her way into the river.

With each tiny step, the feeling of dread faded. Sometimes, she would even try to put all four paws into the water and practice swimming around.

She couldn't go as deep as Serena, the swan, or swim for long periods like the otters, but she was making progress, each step filled with a surge of pride.

But on some days, Lyona found it difficult to overcome the nagging fear.

-Chuck, what if I get caught in a current, or what if I get lost in the water?

- she would worry. She felt the familiar panic creeping in, the knot of dread tightening in her chest.

Seeing her fear, Chuck took a pause.

-I have an idea, - he suggested.

-Sing a song about bravery.

- He began to hum,

-I'm a capybara who's brave, brave, brave. I'm a capybara who's brave. - His song echoed through the stillness of the forest. Lyona, caught by the catchy tune, found her own voice joining in.

-I'm a capybara who's brave, brave, brave! - she repeated, and then,

-I'm not scared of the water anymore! I am not afraid!

The song took her by surprise! Lyona didn't feel as scared anymore. It seemed as if the song had somehow transported her back to that joyful moment by the pond, back to the feeling of swimming with a rainbow shell in her paw, and the way the sunshine danced on the surface.

-That's the spirit! - Chuck chimed in, his voice full of glee,

-You are brave! It's a journey, one small step at a time! But we'll make it together, always.

As Lyona continued singing about bravery, she noticed that she was taking larger and more confident steps. The feeling of panic seemed to have dissipated, replaced by a rush of confidence. She started to notice the joyful songs of birds in the trees, the gentle whisper of leaves, and the rhythm of the water flowing by. She was no longer focused on her fears but on the beauty around her.

Lyona began to believe that facing her fears could also mean celebrating her courage, her joy, and her journey.

Perhaps, just perhaps, one day, she could become like the fearless capybara in Chuck's story, braving the unknown, overcoming the challenges, and ultimately, finding the strength to conquer the currents of fear and reach the calm waters of bravery.

That's what made Lyona believe she was not only going to learn to swim, but become a brave capybara who was also ready to face the world with a smile and a song in her heart.

Chapter 10: Imaginary fish and the fears associated with jumping

Imaginary Fish and the Fears Associated with Jumping

Lyona had taken small, slow steps toward overcoming her fear of water. She was more comfortable near it, even dipping all four paws into the river and slowly practicing small strokes. She wasn't swimming yet, but she felt a huge sense of progress.

She continued practicing with Chuck every day, her confidence slowly growing. But there was one more hurdle that kept her from taking the next big step: she was still scared of jumping into the water. The act of leaping from the edge, that feeling of losing the ground beneath her feet, made her heart pound with fear.

-It's all in your head, Lyona,

- Chuck told her, but even though she knew he was right, the fear remained.

One afternoon, sitting on the edge of the river, watching the water rush by, Lyona began to imagine herself as a fish. A graceful, shimmering fish, sleek and powerful, gliding through the water with effortless grace. She saw herself moving like a flash of silver through shimmering reeds and seaweed, encountering schools of curious fish who welcomed her into their watery world. She pictured the freedom and joy of swimming in the river with confidence.

Her imagination took over, and she started to feel a sense of excitement bubbling within her. If she could be a fish, wouldn't she be leaping in and out of the water, splashing about with pure joy? Her body would be strong, her movements sure. She could even glide through currents with ease!

This fantastical journey in her mind allowed Lyona to feel the excitement of water, instead of just the dread.

She looked down at the river, noticing a pile of colorful leaves gathered on the edge. An idea sparked in her mind! She imagined this pile of leaves was like the edge of a river. It felt like she was on a land where there was no fear associated with falling into the water.

Taking a deep breath, Lyona closed her eyes and with a mighty leap, she flung herself into the pile of leaves, feeling a tiny pang of fear as she left the solid ground. Then she imagined the feel of the cool water embracing her, felt her feet churning and pushing against it. She giggled as she rolled and spun within the soft, warm leaves, pretending they were cool river currents swirling around her.

It felt so much like swimming!

-I'm doing it! I'm doing it! - she shouted in excitement, pushing herself out of the leaves, a small surge of triumph flooding through her.

-It's not so bad after all, - Lyona declared to Chuck who had watched her with a concerned look.

Chuck had never seen Lyona so enthusiastic. It was incredible how quickly the leaves had transformed into an amazing underwater adventure for Lyona.

-Maybe you should try diving into real water now! - Chuck encouraged.

Lyona took a step back, noticing how close the real water was to the bank.

-What if we jump together? - she asked with a brave smile.

-Oh, we definitely should! - Chuck agreed with his usual boundless enthusiasm, even if he already knew how to swim.

And that is how Lyona started to overcome another layer of her fear. Using her imagination to create a joyful and safe space for her fear of jumping. She was inching closer to fulfilling her dreams of becoming a confident capybara, unafraid to dive, swim, and explore the watery world around her.

Chapter 11: Careful Movements and Unexpected Swallows

The next morning, a quiet excitement filled Lyona's heart. After weeks of careful preparation, small steps, and singing brave songs, she was ready for a new adventure: she was going to take her first swim in the river.

Standing on the bank with Chuck beside her, her webbed feet seemed ready to carry her forward. Lyona could hear the river gently murmuring below, a soft music in the silence of the morning air. Her heart was drumming a frantic rhythm.

-Remember, just like we practiced, - Chuck said gently.

-Small steps, and a bit of patience.

-I'm not as scared now, Chuck. Thanks to all your encouragement, and our song of bravery! - Lyona smiled at Chuck, taking one deep breath.

-Okay, here goes!

With a firm grip on the smooth bank, she took one tentative step, followed by another. Then, slowly but surely, she slipped one paw into the cool water, then another. The water, which once seemed so overwhelming, was a gentle wave that welcomed her with a touch of coolness.

-You're doing it! Go, Lyona, go!

- Chuck called, his voice loud with excitement.

She had been imagining this moment for so long! Now, with the strength of her legs and the soft whispers of courage within her, she was about to step into the water, ready to make those strokes and kick!

-Come on, Lyona! - Chuck's voice rang out, encouraging her with his trademark optimism.

-Go, Go!

Lyona smiled, the rush of the water giving her an unexpected surge of energy. She pushed off with one back leg, and with the momentum of the wave, took a joyful leap, and for the first time in her life, she began to swim!

Her heart was bursting with excitement as she moved forward, propelled by her own strength, kicking and reaching for the flowing water, trying to find a rhythm with each stroke.

-Wonderful! Amazing! - Chuck shrieked with delight.

Lyona felt proud. She was swimming! Even though her strokes were uneven and she wobbled, her face glowed with accomplishment, a grin that reached both her tiny ears. She looked around at her surroundings, taking in the trees by the water's edge, the clear sky overhead. The river flowed calmly beneath her.

Lyona looked at Chuck, grinning wide.

-I'm doing it, Chuck! I'm swimming!

-But suddenly, with a mighty gurgle, Lyona swallowed a mouthful of water, causing her to snort in surprise and spit it out. It seemed as if the river was not ready to accept her victory with open arms!

Chuck burst into laughter, even as Lyona gasped,

-Ack! I swallowed some water! I wasn't prepared for that! -

-That's alright!

- Chuck laughed.

-I'll help you remember how to keep your head above the water!

And so, with the rush of victory and a gentle, yet necessary lesson from Chuck about swimming and not accidentally drinking water, Lyona continued to practice her strokes, each stroke bringing her closer to becoming the confident swimmer she always longed to be.

Chapter 12: Webbed feet and uneven breathing

Lyona spent the following days exploring the river with Chuck, feeling more and more comfortable with the water. But with her initial triumph came a new set of challenges. She was no Serena, gliding gracefully. Even with Chuck's help, she struggled with keeping her head above the surface.

-Lyona, look at those paws! - Chuck giggled, looking at Lyona's webbed feet as she stood on the bank of the river.

-Use them to push the water backward! The webs will help you glide, like a powerful otter! That's how I swim! -

Chuck demonstrated with a big splash, showing Lyona how his webbed feet acted like little paddles that allowed him to move through the water.

Lyona tried to mimic his technique, her own paws feeling like oversized flippers as she practiced at the river's edge.

-See! Like this, Chuck?

- Lyona exclaimed, carefully wiggling her paws, imitating his graceful strokes.

-Great! You're catching on fast!

- Chuck cheered, trying to offer her support.

-Let's try this together! I'll help you by gently pushing your back paws! -

Together, Lyona and Chuck swam alongside each other, Lyona trying her best to coordinate her movements. But her webbed feet were just so big and clumsy! She wasn't sure how she was supposed to push through the water without ending up spinning in circles.

-Take a deep breath! - Chuck said, noting Lyona's panic and helping her regain her balance.

And then, there was another problem, something even more difficult to manage.

-Remember what Serena did? - Chuck tried to explain.

-Look at how gracefully she breathes when she's swimming.

Lyona, focusing on her webbed paws, wasn't really paying attention.

-I know, Chuck, it's the best. - She looked up at the sun, and with a great big gasp, she took in a large gulp of air, her lungs suddenly feeling like balloons about to burst!

-I think I'm getting it!

- She sputtered, her head still a little under the water, almost gulping a big swallow!

Chuck swam beside her, looking concerned. He realized Lyona's biggest struggle wasn't actually moving forward in the water, but rather, breathing while swimming!

Lyona looked back at Chuck with a shy grin.

-Do you think I'm okay?

-You're doing great!

- Chuck answered cheerfully.

-But remember: you need to breathe smoothly! Don't be afraid. If you need a break, come up and breathe deeply, so you don't swallow water! Just try to coordinate your movements. -

Lyona continued to swim alongside Chuck, learning to manage her breathing, trying to remember to inhale a breath before her head went under the water. But it wasn't always easy.

Lyona still wasn't sure if she would ever be an accomplished swimmer, like Serena. It seemed she had a whole new set of challenges!

The biggest obstacle remained: the uneven breathing, the panicked gasps, and the feeling of almost swallowing more water than air! She wondered if her fear was winning after all.

Chapter 13: Natural Buoyancy and Exciting Challenges

Despite the occasional panic attacks and big, clumsy breaths, Lyona felt something else. It wasn't just the sun on her fur or the wind rustling the leaves, though they did feel delightful as she floated on the water's surface, breathing deeply and gazing at the clear sky.

She loved the feeling of the water holding her up. Even with all the struggling, the panic, and the feeling of being clumsy, she was swimming. It wasn't the graceful glide she'd pictured for herself. It wasn't a fast sprint like Pedro's. It was more of a bobbing, somewhat wobbly journey, filled with gasps and moments of joy, a lot of funny kicks, and the occasional splash of water in her nose.

But beneath it all, she realized she felt truly alive. It felt good to be able to feel her webbed feet churning through the water, moving with determination.

Lyona couldn't shake the feeling that this wasn't a struggle so much as a challenge. She felt buoyant, a joyous buoyancy. Not the kind Serena displayed with effortless elegance but rather a bobbing buoyancy full of splashes, of surprises, and of laughter. Lyona was finally enjoying her swimming journey.

And it all started with a smile and a word of encouragement from Chuck.

-Come on Lyona! - he cheered,

-You're getting the hang of it!

He looked around for a bright, colorful pebble resting at the river's edge and said,

-How about we make it more exciting?

-We can race!

- Chuck proposed with excitement, pushing the colorful pebble further out into the current, so it rested just beneath the flowing river water.

-Let's try to be the first one to get that bright, colorful stone! What do you think? -

-It looks challenging! - Lyona chuckled, feeling that thrill of adventure pushing her further.

-Just try it, Lyona! - Chuck encouraged her, reminding her to take a deep breath.

Lyona laughed.

-Okay, I'm ready for the challenge! You want to race me to the pebble?! -

-Of course!

- Chuck declared, feeling competitive even though he knew he'd be swimming to the pebble much faster. But he would always wait for Lyona to catch up.

And that is how their adventures continued, with a challenge added with each swimming trip. Sometimes, Chuck would simply try to catch up to Lyona while they swam together. Then he'd come up with different goals: finding specific colored pebbles, or a special river stone, or swimming across the river to a tree on the other side. Lyona, in her determined way, began swimming and exploring with increasing confidence. She even started to dream of the day she would join Serena, Chuck, and other friends in one of their exciting adventures.

That day, Lyona began to enjoy each swim as a moment of pure joy, filled with challenges, discovery, and unbridled joy. It was no longer about avoiding water, but instead about exploring and playing, about discovering how amazing it felt to be afloat!

Chapter 14: Imitation of fish and tips

Lyona was starting to enjoy swimming. She even found that the challenge of trying to catch up to Chuck in a race brought a big smile to her face, even when she knew she'd be swimming far behind.

As Lyona splashed and kicked, a tall heron with elegant, grey feathers perched on the branch of a willow tree overlooking the river, watching with curious eyes. The Heron's long, pointed beak was tucked beneath his wing as he contemplated something with quiet concentration.

Lyona spotted him.

-Hi, Mr. Heron, - she chirped cheerfully.

-You're so tall! I wish I could swim with the grace that you can fly.

-Swimming is as graceful as flying, little Capybara,

- the heron answered in a gentle, soothing voice.

-As long as you find the right rhythm and use the current to your advantage. - He tucked his wings tighter, tilting his head a little, watching the river rush by.

-Did you ever wonder why the fish move the way they do? - he asked curiously.

Lyona hadn't. But as she watched the fish in the clear waters of the river, she found herself marveling at how easy and fluid their movements were, even as the strong currents attempted to pull them around. They would simply glide through the water, their bodies swaying, seemingly dancing as they traversed the rushing water, their tail fins propelling them effortlessly.

The heron pointed a long, delicate wing to a school of little fish.

-Look how they use their fins to push themselves, propelling themselves with swift strokes, - the heron explained.

-But they always try to move along the direction of the flow.

Lyona noticed that the fish, despite moving quickly, seemed to go with the flow of the water. They seemed to avoid any strong force pushing against their body by swaying and following the river's current. They seemed to move effortlessly, their body a reflection of the rushing water.

-Amazing, - Lyona remarked, noticing the beauty of these small creatures gliding and gliding so perfectly through the water. She hoped she could one day move through the water just like they did.

-Try it, Lyona! Let's do it together!

- the heron said, seeing Lyona's amazed expression,

He guided Lyona through some of his techniques: How to position her head when she swims, how to move her body alongside the current rather than against it. It felt odd at first to think about flowing rather than struggling, but as Lyona practiced it with the heron's kind guidance, she felt her fear fade away, replaced by a sense of calmness and focus.

-It's hard to stay balanced, even if I remember to breathe! - Lyona declared with a sigh.

-Oh, balance is a matter of learning how to use the water to help you, my dear Lyona, - the heron said kindly, observing her with wise eyes.

He spread his long wing wide, moving it through the air like a feathered paddle, and demonstrated what he meant by using a bit of the air's current, a kind of gliding movement.

-The water pushes back when we try to push it forward. But if you learn to work with the river's energy, to use its currents to help you along, you will glide so much smoother, - the heron explained.

-That's the key!

Lyona listened attentively, taking a deep breath of the cool, river air. As she practiced, her movements slowly transformed. It felt like magic! Lyona suddenly discovered that swimming felt less like work and more like a delightful journey. She was able to move with more ease and grace.

-Wow, thank you!

- Lyona exclaimed.

-This makes all the difference!

-She decided to listen closely and learn all the tricks from this wonderful bird who moved so effortlessly in the air. And who knew she would be taking lessons from the bird about swimming!

Lyona's adventure in the river was evolving. She felt a lot more balanced and calm, the water didn't seem as daunting. It felt like she had learned a special secret, one that brought her closer to achieving her dream of becoming a true river swimmer.

Chapter 15: Instant Panic and Calm Self-confidence

Lyona was swimming. She wasn't gliding gracefully like Serena, or paddling like a powerful otter. She wasn't quite as quick as Chuck, but she was making progress. Each day brought new discoveries: how to keep her head above the water, how to find the perfect rhythm, how to use the current to her advantage.

She loved the feeling of moving through the river. But there was one thing Lyona still feared - being too far from the shore. The idea of being alone in the water, without the comfort of a solid bank under her feet, brought back a surge of fear, the kind that would bring the feeling of panic, of being out of control, of needing to return to land as quickly as possible.

-Look at you go, Lyona! - Chuck called out from the shore,

- You're getting faster! I can't keep up with you! I'll cheer you on from here! Do you want to try and reach that rock over there? - He pointed to a large rock in the middle of the river.

With a joyous grin and a newfound spirit of adventure, Lyona nodded and decided to go for it. She stroked confidently through the cool water, feeling proud of herself, forgetting for a moment her fears about swimming further away from the bank. The river carried her forward, like an unseen friend helping her along, and suddenly she found herself a good distance away from the bank, surrounded by rushing water. She had never swum so far out, not on her own!

And that's when it happened. Panic rushed through her in a wave. She looked back toward the river bank, and it seemed so far away! It felt like a tiny island in a vast ocean, so distant that she wouldn't be able to reach it.

A moment of terror flashed through her: the cold, murky depths, the imagined grip of the current, the feeling of helplessness, all of her anxieties rushing in like a tide.

She splashed, a confused, frantic series of kicks, but she only moved in circles, struggling to regain control.

-Chuck! I'm afraid! I don't know how to get back!, - Lyona screamed, a tiny plea that barely managed to cross the rushing waters.

-Hold on!

- Chuck's voice rang across the river.

She saw Chuck, with the same calmness she always witnessed, approaching the rock.

-Keep your paws moving! You've done this before! It's just a matter of slowing down your breaths, relaxing those paws, and using those strong legs!

- He had a knowing look on his face, a calm assurance that always worked.

-We'll be there soon! - Chuck reassured, giving her confidence as he slowly glided beside her, guiding her as she caught her breath and started swimming towards the shore with renewed hope. He had taught her how to calm those panics and those anxious moments, a simple mantra of:

-Focus on what you're doing, trust your instincts, and everything will be okay.

Slowly, but surely, she made her way toward the shore.

Once safely back on the bank, Lyona sank her legs into the cool sand, and with a quiet sigh, turned towards her friend.

-Thanks, Chuck, - she said, taking in the beautiful sights around her, and the comforting sound of the flowing river.

-No problem!

- Chuck replied, and he nuzzled Lyona with a reassuring paw.

-You can do it, Lyona! And remember: You've always managed to swim your way back. Don't ever give up! Just keep your eyes on the shore! And remember to breathe!

Chuck, ever the cheerful friend, took the chance to gently teach her another lesson: The importance of not giving up on her goals, even when she was afraid or experiencing challenges. It was his job to remind her of the courage and strength she had found within her own self.

It was a reminder that sometimes the path to our dreams isn't about just conquering our fears, but about the moments we experience as we travel, the people who help us get there, and the knowledge that even when it feels impossible, there will always be someone there to guide us and cheer us on.

Chapter 16: Spreading News and words of encouragement

The news spread through the forest like wildfire: Lyona was swimming! She had conquered her fear of water. It started with Chuck, excitedly telling the other otters during their evening fish hunt.

-Did you hear?! Lyona's swimming now!

The playful otters squealed and laughed, rushing toward Lyona to congratulate her. They all surrounded her on the river bank, their excitement bubbling over.

Then, news of her triumph reached Serena, the swan, gliding majestically across the lake.

-I've heard such wonderful news!

- she announced, her voice calm and sweet.

-You've finally achieved your goal! I'm very proud of you.

-One of the otters, a playful creature called Penny, hopped towards Lyona, her paws tapping rapidly.

-You really are swimming! - she shrieked, grabbing a nearby leaf to wipe a little bit of excitement away from her cheek.

-That's fantastic! I was so scared for you! - She jumped in delight,

-Come on, Lyona, tell us how it went! Tell us everything!

-Yes! Yes! - another playful otter named Jack joined in.

-Is it fun? Tell us about your adventures! We need to know all about how you overcome your fears. -

And that is how Lyona found herself surrounded by her animal friends, all showering her with a torrent of excitement, compliments, and advice. The little capybaras that were there when Lyona was practicing, back in Chapter 7, came forward with a cheer! The otters all took turns trying to show off their swimming skills. The squirrels that used to hide from her when she got scared about being near water started jumping down from trees and hopping playfully on the banks to watch Lyona's adventures in the river.

Lyona felt incredibly proud. And not only that, she felt loved. The love of all the animal friends, from the mischievous otters, to the calm wisdom of Serena, all came together to share their excitement for her. It felt like the biggest hug in the whole forest!

They offered advice. Some otters reminded her to try different strokes, that would improve her technique. Some otters explained the importance of going with the flow, following the river's currents. One wise squirrel pointed to a section in the river that seemed less strong, where she could try new tricks. Even Serena encouraged her to practice her swimming style.

All of them, from the youngest playful creatures to the elders who had watched her with curiosity, were thrilled to hear about Lyona's journey.

-That's exactly how it feels, - Lyona admitted to the group as she took in the warmth of their encouragement, a sense of deep belonging. It wasn't easy to conquer a fear. But there was something really great about the strength you found in the journey, the support of friends and family, the love that bloomed even from the smallest of steps, a warmth you didn't realize could surround you so generously.

-Now, you really are the bravest capybara! - exclaimed Chuck, leading his friends in a chorus of cheering for their amazing friend, the one who swam through fear to the other side!

Chapter 17: Race Strategy and Current Training

The news of Lyona's swimming prowess had reached the ears of the Forest Council, a group of wise animals who organized the annual River Race. And they wanted Lyona to participate.

Lyona, excited but a little apprehensive, received the news with a mixture of nervousness and elation. The race was legendary. It stretched from one side of the forest to the other, along a wide, challenging stretch of the river. The challenge? The river's unpredictable currents and powerful whirlpools. Only the bravest swimmers in the forest participated in the annual race.

Lyona knew the race would be difficult. Even with all the progress she'd made, even with her new swimming style and newfound courage, she wondered if she could ever truly conquer those swift waters. But there was a flicker of courage deep inside, a thrill at the idea of trying, a yearning for that kind of achievement.

Lyona, with a small bit of nervousness, told Chuck all about it.

Chuck was enthusiastic,

-Lyona! We need a strategy! Let's plan this together! -

Chuck grabbed a twig and started drawing a simple diagram on the river bank, mimicking the route of the race,

-We can find a safer path through the river, if you take this side. - Chuck pointed to one section on the river,

-Here we will avoid the dangerous eddies, that's where the fastest currents are. I have noticed it seems the current pulls things backward at times. Maybe it's best to go towards the shore during those times, so that you have the bank to hold on to. -

They began training. Lyona was determined to develop a good strategy, with the support of Chuck and a clear plan. They had to be smart about the way they went against the flow.

Chuck explained to her,

-Think about it: the current moves with the river, we will try and make a small swimming action to counter the movement! A few kicks against the flow, that's the trick, you see!

Lyona practiced. And practiced. She felt she was swimming backwards, not really moving ahead. But she did it, over and over.

She practiced, kicking, swimming against the water flow. She'd practiced even with the leaves as an alternative riverbed. She pushed off with her webbed feet, swimming in a backward direction. It was as if she was climbing uphill, a battle against the current.

The thought of competing, though scary, gave her the strength to continue her training. With every new stroke she practiced against the current, she felt a powerful wave of resilience building inside. Her spirit, just like her swim, felt like it was finally picking up speed.

-We'll do it together, - Chuck assured her,

-I believe in you! And I'll be by your side throughout the race. -

As Lyona swam, practicing to overcome the river's currents, she realized that there were some currents she could overcome through pure physical force. But there were others, she found out, that required strategy, careful observation, and a thoughtful understanding of the path. But mostly, Lyona knew that she'd do it all, with the support and belief of a friend by her side!

Chapter 18: Competitive Spirit and Endurance Laps

The day of the River Race was fast approaching. Excitement pulsed through the air, anticipation filling every nook and cranny of the forest. Capybaras, otters, swans, and even the grumpy river turtles, all gathered at the banks, eager to witness this exciting annual event.

Lyona, surrounded by her friends and surrounded by the energy of all the creatures in the forest, was anxious but filled with a determined spirit. She had practiced relentlessly, building stamina, honing her skills, and overcoming her fears.

She still remembers the moments she stumbled in her training: Swallowing a mouthful of water, those moments of panic when she couldn't see the shore, her wobbly strokes.

But those moments, along with the kindness and support from Chuck, Serena, and all of her animal friends, had only reinforced her spirit. Every step of the way, every lap she completed, each challenge she conquered brought a renewed surge of courage within her.

It was the day of the race. The day to show her skills and prove her strength. She could feel the heartbeats of all her friends. Their love felt as warm as the midday sun as they cheered her on.

The start was loud and chaotic. The river's water splashed in excited, churning motions. Lyona joined the throng of animals who began swimming as fast as their legs could propel them, moving forward into the river's unpredictable waters.

Then she spotted Chuck. Chuck was already racing through the waters like a sleek, powerful otter, gliding with an ease she could only imagine. He moved ahead of the others, easily maneuvering through the tricky current. He even used the powerful currents in a clever way. Chuck would go with the flow, a rhythmic movement, almost a graceful dance, making him seem effortless in his strokes.

It was beautiful!

And it was thrilling! And just a little daunting.

A sudden, unexpected rush of competitive spirit came over Lyona! Her own anxieties seemed to disappear. She, like her swimming, felt herself pick up a bit of speed. Lyona was determined to match her speed and endurance with that of Chuck's, but it wasn't so simple!

There were strong currents that pulled her back, demanding that she work hard. She reminded herself: Don't forget your training, use the techniques, and stay focused on the course. It was an exciting and challenging adventure.

-Hold on! - Lyona thought to herself, pushing with a determined energy. Lyona kicked with her strong webbed feet, channeling the memory of the little fish she'd observed.

There were others who swam next to her, some pushing faster than her. And others who swam slower. But, most importantly, there was one friend by her side who was there to offer advice, a nudge, a reminder that they would be finishing this race, side by side.

For the rest of the race, Lyona kept practicing. She took laps in a different section of the river. She tried different swimming techniques. And then, in her most dedicated training moments, she'd remind herself why she was doing it. She knew that this river wasn't an obstacle to overcome, but instead a powerful element, full of its own magical qualities that she had only just begun to learn about.

Chapter 19: The Owl's Wisdom and Dreams of Victory

As the sun started its descent, casting long shadows across the forest, Lyona decided to rest for the night. The River Race was scheduled for the morning, and she needed all the energy she could muster. But she also needed a clear mind. A wise mind.

Her heart pounded with anxiety. It felt as though it was bouncing like a bouncy ball trapped in a box, an agitated thump against her ribs. Even the trees whispered a melody that matched the pace of her heartbeat! It was hard to relax and try to gain clarity as her fears surrounded her, a chilly cloud over her.

-You're ready, Lyona, - Chuck said softly.

-Don't let fear hold you back. Trust the skills you've learned, the lessons we've had. -

Lyona knew Chuck was right. She needed to find a way to relax her mind and gain a more stable, focused, and determined spirit.

Just as Lyona decided to head back to her grassy bed for a good night's rest, she heard a hoot, deep and soulful, from one of the tallest trees in the forest.

It was the old Owl, his bright, golden eyes peering down from his lofty branch.

-What troubles your heart? - he asked, his voice wise and calm.

-I'm so afraid to race! - Lyona said, taking a deep breath.

-My heart is a racing beat, it's full of nerves! -

-Don't think of fear, dear Lyona,

- the Owl said, peering at her with understanding.

-Remember how we talked about how to avoid those currents. Remember how to work with those powerful flows! Trust those strategies. And trust yourself. -

Lyona looked up at the wise old Owl.

-I know what you mean. But I think of Chuck's speed, of the currents and all those powerful forces... And I'm afraid of failing! I'm afraid of not making it across the finish line.

-Ah, - the Owl said, shifting a bit as he focused on Lyona,

-I believe in you. You can do it. I see a lot of strength within you.

The Owl spoke slowly,

-But the real challenge is this: How do you remain calm? How do you silence all those anxieties?

-What can I do? - Lyona asked, worriedly, her brow furrowed in contemplation.

-It feels so loud inside me. There are all those worries about every single step!

-Quiet those doubts. Remember how the river flows! - The owl pointed a wing, and the moon illuminated his outstretched claw.

-That quiet river! Look how gently it flows. The current may change, but there's something magical about those calm movements! - The owl was trying to calm Lyona's nervous mind.

-So, find your quiet current! Keep the water flowing peacefully in your heart.

Lyona understood.

-Focus. - The Owl reminded her of one of his many important lessons.

-It's important to not let anxieties distract you from your purpose.

With a small, hesitant step, Lyona turned towards the bank.

-Focus, - she repeated to herself as she walked, her footsteps quiet on the path.

And, once she reached the spot of her comfortable grassy bed, she curled up in the comforting softness of the warm, moist earth, breathing deeply. She pictured the race and imagined herself, swimming along, focusing, a rhythmic movement with her webbed paws, following a quiet path. She envisioned a peaceful space, and with those calm thoughts, she drifted into a quiet sleep.

When she dreamt that night, the racing wasn't as wild and daunting as before. In the world of her dreams, it felt joyful, magical. The water didn't frighten her, but encouraged her with its gentle waves and gentle currents, she embraced those currents, becoming a rhythmic, flowing part of the river. She felt strong. She imagined her body gliding, swimming powerfully, as fast as she could! She focused and pushed with all the force she had, her powerful legs pushing the water forward with every stroke! She visualized crossing the finish line first! She felt a surge of excitement, a rush of achievement and pride, that bubbled and fizzed with contentment in her chest.

When she woke in the morning, a calmness she hadn't felt for a long time flooded over her. It felt like an awakening to her spirit, the quiet of her own being! It wasn't magic, but a clear mind. It was that moment she knew that everything she was practicing, every skill she was developing, all her anxieties and doubts, they'd all be brought together for a powerful victory that awaited her.

Chapter 20: Nervous excitement and calm reflection

The air in the forest was thick with anticipation. The River Race was just one day away. Even the leaves seemed to rustle with a little more energy. A buzz of nervous excitement thrummed through the trees.

Everywhere Lyona looked, she saw animals preparing: swans practicing their graceful glide, otters sharpening their swimming skills, and even the river turtles stretching their necks with renewed vigor. But most importantly, there was Chuck.

Chuck was a ball of nerves, bouncing around the bank.

-Are you ready, Lyona? - he squealed, his tiny tail swishing frantically.

Lyona felt nervous. The River Race had never seemed this close before. She took a deep breath, trying to calm her racing heartbeat.

-I think so,

- she said, trying to mask her jitters.

-A little scared but ready!

She decided to take a stroll through the forest, to a quiet patch where a bubbling stream met the edge of the forest.

As she walked, the leaves crinkled beneath her paws and the sun filtered through the branches of trees, creating a gentle play of light and shadow on the forest floor. Lyona sat down at the stream's edge. She loved the gentle whisper of water against the rocks. It was soothing.

-Take it one step at a time, Lyona. - Lyona smiled. That was the Owl's wisdom.

-Don't think about the outcome, the fears of victory and loss. Just think about each movement in the race. Stay calm.

Lyona decided to spend the next hour by herself. The evening was warm, with a soothing, gentle breeze that carried the sweet scents of blooming flowers. She decided to think about the past weeks and her journey, the struggles she'd overcome, the triumphs she'd experienced.

A shy smile filled her heart. The journey to the race, every single one of those days, had filled her with purpose, with challenge, with a newfound confidence. Lyona discovered she wasn't scared of the water anymore. She learned how to love swimming, discovering the beauty of gliding through the river, feeling its current as her guide. And now, she even felt confident to overcome that swift current and reach the end.

Chuck had been her coach. Her therapist. And an amazing friend. The wise old owl taught her valuable lessons about calm and focusing on purpose, even when faced with immense anxiety and doubts.

-It's going to be a great day, Lyona, - Chuck declared.

-You can do this! Remember our strategies!

- He swam up to Lyona's perch at the edge of the stream, giving her a big, playful nudge with his snout.

-Let's try our speed test!

Lyona giggled. The race was only a few hours away! But in those hours, she had the love of all her friends, their advice, and their strength! That felt stronger than any current she'd had to overcome.

Chapter 21: Audience applause and nervousness at the starting line

The morning dawned bright, casting a warm golden light over the entire forest. It was the day of the River Race. Excitement hummed through the air as every creature from every corner of the forest gathered on the riverbank. Capybaras chattered and jostled. The playful otters buzzed around, creating small ripples of delight in the clear water. Even the quiet, majestic swans fluttered their elegant white wings with anticipation.

Lyona, nestled within a sea of furry, feathered, and scaled faces, took a deep breath and glanced at her reflection in the rippling water. The warmth of the sun, the chatter of the crowd, and the thrill of the race all swirled together into a bubbling pot of anticipation, a cauldron of excitement! But her heartbeat, like a small bird trapped within her chest, wouldn't stop drumming in an anxious rhythm.

The starting line seemed further away than ever. A few steps separated her from the water that had been both a fear and a joy, a haven of adventure and discovery. It was about to take her to the finish line, to a victory she dreamt about, to a goal she yearned for, to a challenge that had shaped her soul.

She gazed up and saw all the eyes of the forest on her: the cheerful smiles of otters, the playful, almost teasing glances from squirrels, the watchful gazes of older capybaras. The wise owl stared down from his lofty branch, perched at the highest treetop, his gaze fixed on her.

And she knew she had to trust the Owl's wisdom. Trust her practice. Trust her courage. Trust her friends.

She noticed Chuck swimming by, his little otter tail swishing.

-Ready, Lyona?

- he asked. He had a sparkle in his eyes, an eager expression on his face. It was all about fun and courage.

As the official of the River Race, a wise old turtle, shouted,

-Take your places!

- Lyona shuffled closer, her paws touching the cold, smooth rocks. She placed her big feet firmly on the edge of the starting line, her fur pricked with apprehension. It was right there, only a step from the racing current, and a powerful pull towards the finish line.

The race had begun.

Her friends gave her encouragement, with all the passion that burned in their little animal hearts.

Then, Lyona was surrounded by the noise of the crowd, their enthusiastic shouts, their excited yelps!

-Lyona! You got this!, - the otters shrieked!

-Don't worry! Go for it! We believe in you! - Lyona heard them shout!

-Get ready! Ready, Set, Go! - boomed the old turtle, his voice rumbling from deep within his ancient shell.

The signal had gone off. Lyona was engulfed in a flurry of sound. The nervous thrum of the race vibrated all around her. It had arrived! It was here!

A moment passed and a surge of nervous excitement rushed over her. This was it! This was the big moment! She felt it coursing through her legs, a wild, energetic pull, as though she'd be flung out into the mighty, racing waters.

Taking one step backward, she then looked toward the edge of the bank. The river seemed so deep. She was scared.

-Lyona, - she could hear Chuck's reassuring words in her ear. He'd swam near her, even though the race had started!

-Trust the rhythm. Trust yourself! You are already there!

His words rang in her ear. Lyona felt the soft, moist coolness of the river under her feet. She glanced up and saw Serena and her graceful white wings shimmering on the waters surface. She glanced around, saw all the excited, curious gazes. It felt like the eyes of the forest were watching over her. They'd seen all of her journeys, all her challenges. She realized she was no longer swimming alone. She had a big family here! And all those eyes filled with support made her heart grow ten sizes larger.

With one powerful leap, Lyona joined the River Race!

Chapter 22: The start signal and initial fatigue

The water was cold against Lyona's webbed feet. It felt like a shocking, chilling hug, one she'd learned to adore. It enveloped her as she took her first, powerful, leaping stride. The river current rushed forward. The thrill of the race pushed Lyona forward, carrying her alongside a flood of other courageous, eager swimmers.

The roar of the crowd was like a roaring waterfall. She could hear their chants:

-Go! Lyona! Go! - She smiled and with a burst of determination, kicked off the bank. Her journey to the finish line had finally started.

The excitement was palpable. Lyona felt a bit light-headed, overwhelmed by the surging current, a sudden and unexpected burst of energy, which threatened to push her off her feet.

Lyona remembered how to use her legs, her powerful paws. She had practiced and prepared for this! Lyona began to focus: kicking, propelling her body with all the strength of her strong hind legs, while reaching her front paws through the water in a powerful motion, trying to find that rhythm and keep her body balanced! She looked at Chuck! She felt the strength of the river's current rushing over her! She could see her friends all swimming along! The otters led the way, and some of them had already created an impressive distance between themselves and the rest of the swimmers, showing off those powerful otter-strokes. But there was the heron, that magical heron that taught her how to swim, flying overhead. His grace guided her. He was above, watching over the competition.

It was like a dance! She moved with the river, an exciting dance. The rushing, churning, exciting current became her friend, as she went along, feeling a warmth of belonging, a powerful, joyous feeling! It felt wonderful, invigorating, a magnificent moment in her life, but the river also presented its own challenges. The initial enthusiasm waned, a natural exhaustion took its hold on her small frame. And it was not easy, not at all. The strong current, despite the rhythm of her strokes, seemed to tug and push her body back, attempting to move her backward in the direction she didn't want to go.

-Keep swimming! - Chuck's voice rang across the river, encouraging, urging, and motivating.

The rhythm of the river seemed to calm her body. Her anxieties had transformed into an invigorating kind of calmness, as Lyona continued to move ahead! But there was the current to consider, it moved powerfully in directions Lyona had not intended, attempting to drag her away. The power of this natural force!

-Chuck, - she thought to herself,

-The Owl was right, I do have to work hard! And we do have to practice!

And so, with a rush of excitement and energy, she started to focus, working hard. Every moment felt like she was working against an opponent! The initial momentum and speed of the race faded a little. And she needed a break, a chance to slow down her movements. The powerful waves carried her forward. But she would do it! Lyona's determination grew.

She tried hard to find her own rhythm and her own path through those raging waters, to work in harmony with those powerful forces of nature.

Lyona had trained for the race for so long. The power and grace she had gathered in the weeks preceding it was finally tested by this natural world, these strong forces! She tried hard to find those currents that would help her reach the finish line. And for each step, each stroke she managed to overcome, the rush of success filled her heart with the desire to keep moving! She found her purpose and determination! She would reach the end of the race. She would do it! And she would be strong!

Chapter 23: The roar of the crowd and the unexpected current

Lyona's heart pounded against her ribs like a frantic drummer in a jungle band. The excitement of the River Race swirled around her, carrying her along the current. She moved with a powerful stride, each stroke pushing her forward, fueled by adrenaline and a new burst of energy.

She caught a glimpse of Chuck in the swirling water. He moved with effortless grace, guiding himself with the rhythm of the river. His brown fur seemed to gleam beneath the light of the midday sun, a shimmering otter with remarkable skill! It made her want to go faster, to work harder, and she almost lost track of the competition, forgetting to breathe.

The cheer of the forest audience came as a comforting melody to Lyona's ear.

-Go Lyona! Go Lyona!

- the crowd shouted.

-You've got this! We believe in you!

Chuck, who had been leading, had caught up to Lyona.

-I'm just trying to make you feel a little bit of the pressure! - he chuckled.

-I'm really just looking out for you! -

Chuck's humor eased her anxiety.

-I'm a little worried! - Lyona said with a laugh.

-You can do it!

- Chuck exclaimed, guiding his nose beneath hers, in a light gesture of reassurance. They both tried to gain an edge, working hard. It became an almost playful dance.

Suddenly, with a sudden burst of momentum, the current, the source of the rhythm of this mighty river, pushed forward, creating a wild, untamed ripple that flung Lyona backwards, turning her head against the water. It almost felt like she was drowning!

For a moment, panic overwhelmed Lyona. She had to struggle to maintain her balance, her body, suddenly off course! The crowd's joyful cheers transformed into gasps of anxiety and worry!

-I'm going to be swept away! - Lyona panicked. She remembered how to keep herself calm and the calm rhythm she'd worked so hard to find.

She felt that she had been knocked off course. The strong, unyielding force of the river.

-Whoa!

- Chuck shrieked, also caught by the current! They were swept a bit off course, carried forward with a powerful current!

Lyona tried to regain her composure and tried to regain the steady rhythm of her strokes, But her panic wouldn't ease so easily.

Lyona took a deep breath. She tried to slow down those rushed gasps.

-Don't worry, - she reminded herself.

-Stay focused. Don't panic.

- Lyona knew this! The Owl, Chuck, and even those wild, powerful currents of the river had taught her to stay strong, to remain centered! But, the fear of being swallowed by the current lingered within her.

Lyona knew she was in danger. She needed to find the balance. The gentle currents of the river, the one's she knew how to dance with, were gone! They'd disappeared. She felt so vulnerable!

Chapter 24: Course Correction and the Last Leap

Lyona was lost in the wild swirl of the powerful currents, a capybara adrift, swept away by the forceful river.

-Think! - she said to herself, the roar of the crowd blending with her own heartbeat, which pounded in her chest as though it were a frantic drum! The anxiety that gripped her felt powerful, it threatened to steal away her courage.

She remembered how she used to fear this river. But she remembered Chuck's calm instructions, his unwavering reassurance that she could swim, his belief that her anxieties were always overcome with a gentle, thoughtful voice,

-Slow breaths. Calm breaths.

She remembered the owl's lessons about the rhythm, the calm, steady river that needed to flow inside.

-This current, - she thought,

-it's not a villain! It's a force that demands respect! I need to dance with the current! I need to embrace the rhythm of this incredible force! -

The river tried to guide her, pushing, pulling, challenging!

-Go Lyona! - the river's water seemed to say, and Lyona followed the flow of its gentle, powerful rush, swimming towards the current, rather than fighting it.

And, suddenly, with that change, that mindful change, it all made a difference! Her fear vanished! She moved forward, almost gliding, with the river as her guide.

-Chuck! We are okay! Look at that current! - Lyona almost screamed in surprise. As if from out of nowhere, she saw Chuck alongside her, looking strong and confident. He too, was going with the flow, trusting those strong currents to propel him forward, making an amazing move toward the end! It felt exhilarating!

Lyona continued to use the currents. She looked at the crowd.

-This is my time, she thought to herself, my moment, my journey.

The audience cheered louder as the animals reached the final stretch of the River Race, where the competition was at its strongest, where they had to overcome the fastest waters to reach the end.

-You are doing so well! - Chuck said. They were close now.

-We're going to cross the finish line together.

She pushed hard. Lyona noticed those few capybaras in the race still remained, their strength seemed almost unwavering! She didn't give up, she knew this would be a battle till the very last stroke!

Lyona knew that one last leap was ahead of them. A sudden, magnificent effort to reach the end. She could hear the excitement of the audience, the chanting of the forest that cheered as each animal pushed for those final moments! She saw Chuck swimming alongside her. They had arrived together. They were both so close!

Lyona had overcome a journey that tested her. She'd battled a flood of anxious waves, a few near-drownings. But, there were always gentle waters that kept her flowing.

Lyona realized that she was not a fearful capybara, who could not overcome the power of water. She was not scared of her journey or her dreams anymore! Lyona felt as if she had begun to conquer something even bigger, something even grander.

That was the true journey. She had found a kind of self-belief that had filled her spirit with such strength, determination, and joy!

Chapter 25: The Finish line and the joy of swimming

The Finish Line and the Joy of Swimming

A great wave of exhilaration pulsed through Lyona. Her paws pushed through the rushing water, and she glided across the finish line. Chuck, close by her side, swam next to her, his tiny otter face grinning with excitement.

-We did it! - he yelled.

-We actually made it to the end! -

It was as if her body moved with a gentle pulse, one that came with a joyful heart and the courage she discovered through the challenges of her journey.

The forest erupted into cheers as every animal gathered on the banks, their voices rising in a collective, glorious crescendo!

-I can't believe we made it!

- Lyona gasped, as though the moment were something unreal, as if it was an improbable journey, a triumph that defied imagination.

-You were incredible, Lyona! You truly learned how to overcome your fears, and now you are an expert swimmer! - Chuck's words were like sweet nectar to Lyona's ears!

Then, just as she felt a warmth of pride blossom within her heart, a hush came over the crowd as the official turtle, with a dignified grace, held up a piece of bark, which was a picture of two swimming forms that captured a precise moment, a snapshot of a single second as those forms touched the finish line. It was a close race! And that image captured that magic of that moment, the incredible closeness of this moment.

It was a photo finish! The forest fell silent, the suspense creating an unbearable weight in the air! Lyona had lost. By the thinnest of margins, she was overtaken by a speedy Beaver. Lyona's dream of winning, though not accomplished, was still remarkable!

-Lyona! That was an incredible journey! The most magnificent, effortful journey! - Serena said, joining the crowd, Her white wings created a lovely shimmering in the waters as she came to reassure her.

Chuck was so very proud.

-Lyona, that was amazing! You swam the river!

Lyona smiled, remembering the beginning. The journey was long, but she found her strength, her calm, her grace in that time.

The crowd erupted again with thunderous applause for all those who made it. Lyona listened, her heart beaming as every creature shouted! It seemed the entire forest cheered, a burst of joy that made her feel so loved. She'd learned to face her fears, embrace her strength, and believe in herself! The forest had celebrated every journey!

But then the crowd gave an extra special applause for one of the creatures. They yelled,

-The Beaver! The Beaver!

That little creature, that incredible creature was a phenomenal swimmer!

A wise old owl announced,

-The winner! Beaver! - and the crowd applauded his effort! The forest cheered, as if that small furry creature had flown to the top of the clouds and returned in that exciting moment! It seemed they were all mesmerized, taken by the powerful surge of victory that surrounded the winner!

Lyona watched on. It filled her heart with a peaceful acceptance, a realization that those powerful currents, her fears and uncertainties, were still a journey ahead of her!

-It wasn't about the winner, Lyona, - said Chuck.

-You're the real victor in all of this, don't you agree! You swam through it all. - His encouragement reminded her of that inner victory, the joy she felt as she completed the journey of the River Race, that calm within that came as she overcame her greatest fears.

Lyona knew. It had all begun in that little mud puddle, and the moment that she first began swimming, her world transformed! The challenge she'd faced, the courage she'd found. Lyona realised that sometimes, to conquer, you don't need to win but to simply participate, to keep on going, even when there are doubts, moments of panic, and uncertain currents.

She glanced at Chuck. His excitement beamed as if there was a light shining bright! She could hear a rumble in his chest that showed that the journey had meant everything to him as well!

As Lyona sat back down on the river bank, looking at the sun, her heart filled with that warmth that came with realizing her true achievement. She no longer was the capybara who had feared water, She now loved swimming.

Don't miss out!

Visit the website below and you can sign up to receive emails whenever Max Marshall publishes a new book. There's no charge and no obligation.

https://books2read.com/r/B-A-DLFY-ZORFF

BOOKS 2 READ

Connecting independent readers to independent writers.

Did you love *Capybara Learning to Swim*? Then you should read *Apocalyptic Time Jump: Clone Attack*[1] by Max Marshall!

[2]

Children's Book in rhyming story for kids from 3 to 8 years. Tale in verse. 60 pages with text and colorful picture.

Once upon a time, in a world much like our own, there lived a curious boy named Max. One fateful day, Max stumbles upon a mysterious time machine hidden in the depths of his backyard, whisking him away to a post-apocalyptic future. To his shock and dismay, Max discovers that in this desolate world, he has a clone named Miller who is wreaking havoc and causing chaos among the peaceful inhabitants. Faced with the daunting task of clearing his name and righting the wrongs committed by his clone, Max embarks on a thrilling adventure to find Miller and put an end to his malevolent deeds. Will Max be able to stop his mischievous clone and restore peace to the future world? Join Max on an unforgettable journey of self-discovery, courage, and redemption in this gripping children's fairy tale of bravery and friendship.

1. https://books2read.com/u/b6aDN6
2. https://books2read.com/u/b6aDN6

Milton Keynes UK
Ingram Content Group UK Ltd.
UKHW012301141124
451095UK00011B/170